A Dream of Danger

by
Kirsty White

Illustrations by Hamesh Alles

W

FRANKLIN WATTS

LONDON • NEW YORK • SYDNEY

A Dream

**This book is to be returned on or before
the last date stamped below.**

First published in 1997 by Franklin Watts

This paperback edition published in 1998

Franklin Watts
96 Leonard Street
London EC2A 4RH

Franklin Watts Australia
14 Mars Road
Lane Cove
NSW 2006

Editor: Kyla Barber
Series editor: Paula Borton
Designer: Kirstie Billingham
Consultant: Douglas Ansdell

A CIP catalogue record for this book
is available from the British Library.

ISBN   0 7496 3124 4 (pbk)
       0 7496 2587 2 (hbk)

Dewey Classification 941.106

Printed in Great Britain

1

The Nightmare Begins

It was the depths of winter and the wind
howled like a banshee. Morag was
awakened by a dream. As usual, she could
not remember what it was about, only that
it had frightened her. She lay in the
darkness of her aunt's cottage in Glencoe,

listening to the storm outside, wondering
when the weather would clear so that she
would be able to go home.

Morag was the granddaughter of Niall,
Chief of Clanranald. For a while now she
had been troubled by bad dreams and her
parents thought that it might help if she
stayed with her Aunt Mary in Glencoe.
They thought a change of scenery would be

good for her. The castle back in Moidart was gloomy – haunted, it was said, by many ghosts.

Morag lay in the darkness, trying to work out what it was that had frightened her so. She'd been having the same dream over and over again since the start of the summer. And since she'd come to Glencoe, it had become worse.

The times were troubled. King James was exiled, and there was a new king, William, on the throne of England and Scotland. Morag's grandfather wasn't happy about it, nor were most of the other highland clans. They had fought for King James, but they'd been defeated at the battle of Cromdale, two years before.

Morag couldn't see what difference it made, the King was in London, many hundreds of miles away. What did it matter who was King?

She heard a rustle beside her. Aunt Mary stood there with a cup of warm milk.

"You look troubled," Aunt Mary said. "Were you dreaming again?"

Morag said nothing. She didn't want to talk about her dreams. She thought that if she ignored them they might go away.

Aunt Mary sat down on the bed beside her and brushed the tangled hair from Morag's forehead. "You know, Morag, your dreams might be the Sight. It runs in your family."

Morag shivered. The thought that her dreams might come true scared her. If she did have second sight, all she could foresee was danger.

The next morning, after breakfast,
Morag wrapped her shawl around her and
went out. Although the weather was bitterly
cold, the winter sun was shining brightly, the
sky icy blue against the white-
capped mountains. The wind
had brushed the snow
into drifts and the
sheep struggled to
find grass to eat.

As Morag passed the Chief's house, she heard a shout, then she saw Iain, his son, waving to her. She smiled at him as he walked towards her.

"Father's back," he said. "He signed the oath."

All of the chiefs had to pledge their loyalty to King William. Morag knew that MacIan had been putting it off.

"Did your grandfather sign, do you know?" Iain asked her.

Morag shook her head. "I don't know. I only know he didn't want to."

Iain smiled. "It's easy for you. You've got the islands. We're only a few miles from the Redcoats at Fort William."

11

"Redcoats?" Morag said. Something about the word troubled her.

"William's soldiers," Iain said. "Campbells and their ilk."

The Campbells of Argyle, unlike the MacDonalds of Glencoe, supported William. The MacDonalds didn't trust them.

Suddenly, they heard a piercing whistle.

"What's that?" Morag asked.

"It's Donald," Iain said. "He's watching the pass.

There must be someone coming."

They ran along the path until they reached the rock that overlooked the road. Donald, Iain's brother, was watching intently.

"Who is it?" Iain asked him.

Donald stood aside. "See for yourself."

Iain looked and saw a group of red-coated figures riding up the track. Behind them there was a column of men on foot. As they came closer, Iain saw that all the men were armed.

"Redcoats," he said. "Soldiers."

"What do they want with us?"
Donald asked. "Father's signed the oath."

"I don't know," Iain said.

Morag looked over Iain's shoulder,
then she gasped. There was something
familiar about the soldiers, something that
frightened her, although she did not know
what it was.

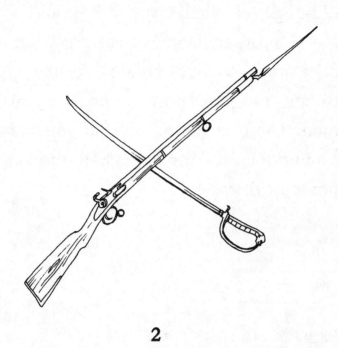

2

Unwelcome Guests

MacIan, the Chief, cursed softly. "A
hundred and twenty men to shelter and
feed," he said, "and horses as well."

"We can't let them go hungry," Janet,
his wife, said.

"Of course not," MacIan said,

although secretly he wished he could.

Morag and Iain watched as MacIan gave orders to make bedding for the troops, and Janet bustled about organising food. The Redcoat officers sat on stools around the fire, drinking ale and talking amongst themselves.

"I don't like it," Iain said under his breath.

Morag struggled to smile. She didn't want him to see that she did not like it either. Suddenly, her Aunt Mary appeared. "Come on," she said to Morag, "you'll have to help me bake for them."

Morag said goodbye to Iain and followed her aunt to the cottage. They spent all day cooking. Morag was very tired that night, but the thought of the troops in the barn kept her awake. When at last their candle went out, she fell asleep.

The dawn was crisp and dry with hardly a breath of wind. Aunt Mary opened the door of the cottage and looked out. The mist had cleared and in the distance she could see the rise of the mountains, miles away on the other side of the glen.

"The weather's fine," she said. "If it stays like this you can go home soon."

Morag said nothing. She did not want
to leave until the Redcoats were gone,
until she was sure that the danger she
sensed was just in her imagination.

"There's no sign of them leaving," Aunt
Mary said as she turned towards the barn,
as if she knew what Morag was thinking.

Morag joined her at the door. "I don't
like them," she said.

"Nobody does," Aunt Mary said.

"I'm afraid of them," Morag said carefully.

"Tush, lass, there's no need to be. They might be Redcoats, but the war's over. They'd not hurt us."

Morag went to the fireside, where the porridge had been cooking slowly overnight.

She helped herself to a bowlful, then spooned out a bowl for Aunt Mary.

As they finished eating, they heard a drumbeat, then a high-pitched tune that Morag had never heard before. They rushed to the door and saw that the Redcoats were drilling, marching up and down to the beat of a drum as a young lad played a whistle. The music sounded odd to Morag, who was used to the sound of bagpipes.

Suddenly Donald appeared with some of his friends. They took one look at the band of soldiers,

and then began to march behind them,
mimicking their stiff strides. Attracted by the
noise, MacIan's hunting dogs began to
howl, drowning out the sound of the whistle
and the drum.

The soldiers faltered, lost the beat and began to bump into each other. Morag could not help it. She burst out laughing, and so did Aunt Mary and everyone else who was watching.

The soldiers stood in a sullen knot, furious at being mocked. Donald yelled something rude about King William and then ran off before any of the Redcoats could catch up with him, but they didn't try particularly hard.

"See?" Aunt Mary said. "They're absolutely harmless."

3

Friends or Foes?

In the evening the women fed the soldiers
on roast mutton. Afterwards there was a
ceilidh in the chief's house. MacIan served
ale generously but only poured small
drams of the whisky he distilled himself.
He'd not paid excise duty on it. He said

the government had a terrible cheek to charge
a man for something he made himself.

Robert Campbell, the Redcoats'
commanding officer, drank his dram quickly
and then asked for more.
As the Redcoat drank
his fill, MacIan
muttered sourly
that now he'd
paid his tax in full.

A singer sang a song about a woman who fell in love with the ghost of a warrior, and then Tormod Og, the clan's bard, told funny stories  about days gone by. Morag listened, laughing, but when she looked around she saw that the soldiers' faces were straight and then Tormod's stories didn't seem funny any more.

The ceilidh finished early. The night was brightly lit by the moon, the mountains brilliant-white against an ebony sky. As she walked back to the cottage with Aunt Mary, Morag felt faint all of a sudden and the landscape melted into a blur.

She blinked to clear her vision, then she felt a sense of danger so intense that she shivered.

Aunt Mary gripped her arm. "If we run, you'll not feel the cold."

The cottage was lit softly by a fire that glowed in the hearth. Aunt Mary made the bedding ready whilst Morag tried to warm herself by the peats, but the chill did not leave her.

"Whatever's the matter, pet?" Aunt
Mary asked her. "You're as white as a ghost."

Morag sat down on a stool and took
a deep breath. "We're in danger, terrible
danger," she said. "The Redcoats, they're
going to kill us."

Aunt Mary looked at her for a moment
and then she knelt beside her, taking
Morag's hand in her own. "MacIan signed

the oath, pet.
William's soldiers
aren't our enemies
any more."

Morag shook
her head. "They're
going to kill us."

"Why d'you
say that?"

Morag
could not find
the words to explain.
It was a feeling she had rather than a reason.

"If they were going to hurt us," Aunt
Mary said, "they'd have done it right away.
We'll have to learn to live with them,
Morag. It's harder to make peace than it is
to make war. The hardest thing of all is to
make friends with our enemies, but we
have to or the war would go on for ever and

we can't have that, can we?"

Morag managed a weak smile. Aunt
Mary stood up
and made her
a cup of warm
milk with honey.
Then Morag
went to bed,
where she lay
and watched
the passage
of the moon.

She did not
sleep that night.
It wasn't that
she was afraid
to dream, she was trying to remember what
her dreams were about. Aunt Mary had
said that her dreams might be the Sight
and if they were then Morag could foretell

danger, but when she told Aunt Mary that she sensed that the Redcoats meant to harm them, Aunt Mary told her that she was imagining things.

Morag didn't know much about the Sight, only that people who had it felt that it was a curse as much as a blessing.

"Never trust a Campbell or a Redcoat," Morag's grandfather had often told her. The soldiers staying in the glen were both.

Morag couldn't work out whether her fear of them was real, or just in her mind.

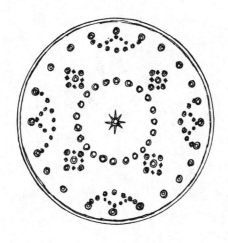

4

Facing the Danger

In the morning, when the Redcoats drilled again, Donald stood there watching. His father had told him not to make a fool of them again, because it was bad manners.

Morag tried to ignore them, but with the racket they made she couldn't, and

so she watched with the others. Aunt Mary
had said nothing about their talk last night
and Morag knew that she did not want to
remind her about it. When the drumbeat
stopped and the soldiers stood rigidly to
attention, she asked Aunt Mary how she
would know if she had the Sight.

"Whatever makes you ask that, pet?"
Aunt Mary said to her.

"It's just that you said these dreams, they might be the Sight."

"Tush, pet, don't you go worrying yourself. If you had the Sight, you'd know all about it, for sure."

Morag was relieved, because she wasn't sure, and that meant that she didn't have it.

Later, the soldiers began to practise tossing the caber and Iain and some of the other boys joined them. Morag stood watching, egging Iain on, proud that he could toss the caber higher and further than the Redcoats although he was much younger than them. He saw her watching him and he winked at her and then smiled, and Morag felt happy for the first time in days. She was so happy that when a young Redcoat smiled shyly at her, she grinned back at him.

The Redcoat nodded towards Iain. "Is he your brother?"

Morag shook her head. "We're not related."

"You're not from Glencoe, then? What are you doing here?"

"I'm a Clanranald. My aunt's the widow of Angus MacDonald and I'm staying with her."

The soldier said nothing for a moment and then he asked her when she was going home. Morag said that she didn't know, and then her attention was diverted by an excellent toss by Iain.

Once the game ended, she gave Iain a cup of *stapag*, an oatmeal drink that her aunt made when the weather was cold.

He drank it and then he thanked her and they walked away from the group of soldiers.

"When are they going?" she asked him.

"They're waiting for orders from Fort William." Iain smiled. "I've a mind to forge a letter telling them to go, but I doubt they'd believe it."

Morag laughed. Iain looked at the dark clouds gathering in the sky above the glen.

"There's a storm coming. If they left now they'd get stuck in it." He said with a grin.

"That's too much to hope for."

She sighed.

Snow started to fall that afternoon.
By night-time, the cottage was almost
buried. As they ate dinner, the wind
howled outside and Aunt Mary said they'd
best get to bed early, because the only
thing to do in weather like that was to
sleep through it.

Morag was exhausted. She'd had no sleep the night before. Her last thought before she closed her eyes was that there was nothing sinister in the soldiers' presence. They were just waiting for their orders, that was all.

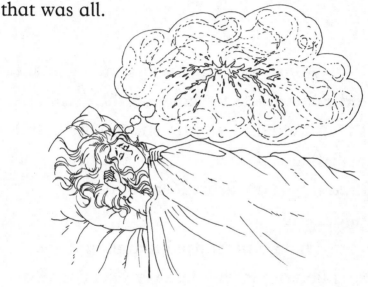

The dream started. At first Morag felt only dread. The shapes she saw weren't clear, just misted whorls with darkness at their core. Then the darkness began to glow with red that dripped like blood from a wound.

Morag opened her eyes then, but she did not struggle to shake off the dream as she usually did. Instead she lay there and willed herself back to sleep, because, if her dream was a warning, she had to understand it.

The dream started again, and she was floating in the sky over Glencoe. The valley itself was covered in darkness.

Morag willed herself to have the courage to face the danger. At first she saw nothing but shadows, but as she gazed at them the shadows sharpened into

shapes that she recognised. She could see
Aunt Mary's cottage, at the edge of the
glen, and then the cottages that belonged
to the clansmen and the slightly bigger
house where MacIan lived, next to the barn
where the Redcoats were sleeping.

Although it was night, the barn was
lit by candles, and inside Morag could see
that the soldiers were fully dressed, holding
their weapons as if they were about to go
into battle.

She woke up then, and remembered everything. The people of the glen were in terrible danger. Trembling, Morag got up and pulled a skirt on over her nightgown. Aunt Mary was deeply asleep in her own bed. Morag looked at her for a moment before deciding not to wake her. Instead, she went out herself to make sure that what she had dreamed was real.

The snow was so thick that she could hardly see the path. She wound her shawl around her shoulders and then set off blindly, heading in the direction of the barn.

It was as she'd foreseen, lit by candlelight which spilled out in yellow streaks across the snow. Although she dared not go close enough to see what the soldiers were doing, above the sound of the wind she could hear them talking.

Morag turned and ran to MacIan's house, where she found Iain at the door.

He smiled when he saw her, as he always did. "I couldn't sleep," he said. "I don't trust the Redcoats, whatever they say."

Morag gulped and told him about her dream. Iain listened carefully and then he told her to wait while he went to see what was going on.

In a moment,
he was lost in the storm.
Morag held her breath until he came
back with a face as white as the snow.

"They're going to attack now,"
he said tersely. "That story about
waiting for orders, it was a lie.
They've had their orders
all along."

Morag
thought for a
moment, telling
herself to be
sensible, that to
panic would
not help.

"I'll tell them I'm Clanranald's granddaughter," she said. "If they attack you, they'll have to answer to him."

Iain shook his head. "No." He said. "At best, they'd just take you prisoner. Go and warn the women while I wake my father."

A muffled noise sounded.
They turned and saw that
the door of the barn had
opened and a column
of soldiers was marching
towards them.

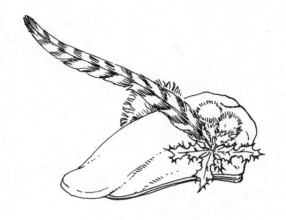

5

Into the Storm

Iain ran indoors as Morag raced back to the cottage. Her aunt did not question her. She got up and dressed quickly and then they went to wake the others. The men ran to MacIan's as the women and children headed for the path that led out of the glen.

"I should've listened to you," Aunt Mary said to Morag as they struggled through snowdrifts that were as deep as they were tall. "I'm sorry."

Morag smiled sadly. "Don't be. I didn't believe it myself."

Aunt Mary looked at her. "You had the courage to face your fear, Morag."

Morag said nothing.

The storm eased a little, and the women found a cave in which they hid.

Although they were cold and tired, they were safe there from the Redcoats. Everyone knew that something terrible had happened and rather than talk about it they were silent.

Suddenly, Morag knew that Iain was in danger. Before anyone could stop her, she ran out of the cave, into the storm. The weather was so bad she could not see the path, although she heard Aunt Mary's cries, telling her to come back.

Morag yelled that she wouldn't be long, and then she began to run, tilting her shoulders into the gale. The wind was so strong that a couple of times she was nearly blown down, but she kept on, because she knew that she would never forgive herself if she didn't try to help Iain.

She found him halfway up the glen,
carrying Donald over his shoulder. The
Redcoats were only yards away.

Iain tried to grab Morag, but she
avoided him and faced the soldiers with
a look so fierce that they stopped dead.
Then they raised their swords threateningly.

"Don't!" she yelled. "My grandfather's Clanranald. If you harm me, he'll not forgive you."

The soldiers looked at each other.

"Stand aside," one of them said, "we're not finished with the MacDonalds yet."

Morag did not move.

"Go away," Iain hissed. "Go now while you've got the chance."

Morag ignored him and took a step towards the Redcoats. Their swords were red. With horror, she realised that the red was blood. Her mind was whirling. What could she do?

They were standing at the place where Donald had first seen the Redcoats a few days before. The path was level at that point, before it dipped sharply towards the glen. The hillside was very steep and covered with deep snow. Even the rock that they had hidden behind was almost buried.

Morag glanced at the rock, and thought that if she could push it at the Redcoats, then she might be able to knock them over and gain a few precious minutes.

Iain tugged at her arm. Roughly, she pushed him away. With the weight of Donald, Iain tumbled and fell off the path, but Morag knew that the snow would soften his fall.

The Redcoats lunged towards her. Morag murmured a prayer, then slipped

behind the rock and pushed with all
her might.

The Redcoats did not see where she'd
gone, they headed off down the path,
calling out to her.

For a moment, the rock did not
move, then Morag felt it give a little.
She pushed again, as hard as she could,
almost crying out with the effort.

The rock moved a little more and then it began to roll down the path towards the soldiers, gaining speed as it neared them.

The rolling rock disturbed the freshly fallen snow, setting off a small avalanche that grew bigger as the snow slid down the hill.

Morag watched, hardly daring to breathe.

The torrent of snow and rock hit the Redcoats from behind. They yelled out with alarm and pain, but the avalanche buried them, stifling their cries.

Morag did not wait. She only had a moment before the soldiers would be on their feet again, looking for her. She ran down to Iain and helped him to carry Donald to the cave.

Iain said nothing until they reached safety. As Aunt Mary tended Donald's cut shoulder, Iain said that his father and at least three dozen more men were dead, and several more injured.

His grief was deep in his eyes.

"Morag saved my life," he said.
"And Donald's, and everyone else who's here."

Morag looked away. "If only I'd
known sooner," she said.

They still had to get out of the glen and
although the storm eased from time to time
the clouds were so thick that they knew the
bad weather would last for days.

Morag slipped away and, hidden by
the mist, went to the village where she
heard the soldiers singing drunkenly now
that the killing was done.

Silently, she untethered Robert
Campbell's horse and then mounted it and
rode it away, leading the other horses by
their reins.

The thought that the Redcoat officers would have to walk back to Fort William cheered the MacDonalds and Morag a little, as they headed for the safety of Clanranald's land.

◆

In time, the MacDonalds who had survived the massacre returned to the glen. They fought bravely against the English in every battle until the terrible defeat at Culloden.

After that, the glen lost its people and became the empty place that it is today. But it is said that the ghosts of the MacDonalds killed by the Redcoats still roam there. Although more than three hundred years have passed since the massacre, the people of Scotland have not forgotten the dead of Glencoe, nor have they forgiven those responsible for it.

The Massacre of Glencoe

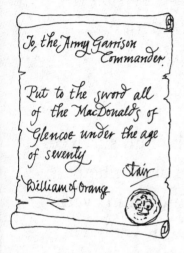

To, the Army Garrison
Commander

Put to the sword all
of the MacDonalds of
Glencoe under the age
of seventy

Stair

William of Orange

The massacre was planned by John Dalrymple, a government minister. The MacDonalds of Glencoe were chosen as victims not only because their chief MacIan had been late in signing the oath of loyalty to King William, but also because they were thought to be disobedient and lawless. When Dalrymple's orders were passed to the army commander, they carried the signature of the King himself.

Although there have been many bloody incidents in Scottish history, the Glencoe massacre horrified the whole nation. The troops were ordered to kill all the MacDonalds under the age of seventy, including women and children, although they actually killed only 38 people.

The majority of the MacDonalds escaped, although some died in the terrible storm that swept through the glen that day.

The Glorious Revolution

The Glorious Revolution is the
name given to the victory of King
William of Orange, the nephew of
King Charles II, over forces loyal to
King James VII, who went into exile in 1689.
William was popular with English Protestants and
most Lowland Scots. But the Highlanders and many
Irish refused to accept his right to the throne and
continued to support the exiled King James. They
became known as 'Jacobites'.

The Bards

Gaelic-speaking people have great respect for learning.
But paper (parchment) was expensive
and, without printing presses, book
production by hand was a slow
process. So each clan had a bard,
who passed on history in the
form of oral stories and
acted as a 'living book'.

It was the bard's job to record the achievements of the clan, to write slogans to spur the clansmen on in battle, and to celebrate their victories in verse. The bards were so powerful that many English governments tried to ban them.

Second Sight

There are many stories in Scottish history of people who have been able to foretell the future. This ability is feared, because the future is sometimes frightening, as it was for Morag. In the past, every village had a seer. The commonest visions were of death and disaster. The most famous Scottish seer was Coinneach Odhar, the Brahan Seer. Amongst other things, he foresaw the building of the Caledonian canal, railways and aeroplanes.